Animated Classics

Disney

The Lion King

studio fun
INTERNATIONAL

Studio Fun International
An imprint of Printers Row Publishing Group
A division of Readerlink Distribution Services, LLC
10350 Barnes Canyon Road, Suite 100, San Diego, CA 92121
www.studiofun.com

Printers Row Publishing Group is a division of Readerlink Distribution Services, LLC.
Studio Fun International is a registered trademark of Readerlink Distribution Services, LLC.

All notations of errors or omissions should be addressed to Studio Fun International,
Editorial Department, at the above address.
Special thanks to the Walt Disney Animation Research Library staff for providing the artwork for this book.

ISBN: 978-0-7944-4555-3
Manufactured, printed, and assembled in Dongguan, China.
First printing, October 2019. RRD/10/19
23 22 21 20 19   1 2 3 4 5

This book belongs to

*T*he Lion King hit theaters in June 1994. I was eight years old and already had a healthy love of drawing, inspired largely by Disney's library of animated films. But something about this movie was different for me. Before the movie was even released, I saw the trailer in theaters, and it stuck with me for a long, long time.

I can't recall any one reason that *The Lion King* resonated with my young self as much as it did. Perhaps it was the music, or the rich visuals, or the fact that it transported me to a place that no fairy tale had up to that point. The emotions of the film, the choices the characters make, and the journey they go on certainly touch something inside all of us. I'm sure the talking animals were a big selling feature for me as well. But I do recall feeling, although the exact thought wasn't fully formed in my head, "I want to make something like this."

It didn't take long for that thought to crystalize. I was nine years old when I saw a behind-the-scenes TV special about rough animation, saw an animator flipping sheets of paper, and it clicked for me: "Oh! You can make a movie with drawings!" I knew then that I wanted to work in animation.

I spent hours poring through the Art of The Lion King book. I studied the different art styles until I could name the artist just by looking at a drawing. Seeing the names of female story artists, such as Lorna Cook and Brenda Chapman, was no doubt of great significance, but I had no idea how noteworthy that was at the time.

It's a bizarre and beautiful thing to have wound up with the job I wanted when I was nine. I've had the pleasure of knowing and working with some of the people whose names I memorized from that art book. Much about the way we make movies has changed, but the core of the films, the artistry and storytelling—all the things that make *The Lion King* the masterpiece it is—is still here in spades. I hope anyone reading this book finds their "Lion King" and is inspired to go out and make awesome things.

Lissa Treiman
Walt Disney Animation Studios

*T*he sun rose over the savannah, huge and yellow in the vast sky.

All the animals in the kingdom raised their heads to the sun. Then, as one, they began to move. Impalas leaped, zebras galloped, and elephants swayed across the plains. Large and small, they swam, flew, and marched to Pride Rock, where Mufasa, their king, stood proudly.

The crowd of animals parted to make way for Rafiki, a friend and advisor of the royal family. He climbed Pride Rock until he reached Mufasa, and then hugged him.

Mufasa smiled and strode over to his wife, Sarabi. Nestled in her paws was their tiny cub.

Rafiki smeared red juice and scattered dust across the cub's forehead. Then he carried the cub to the edge of Pride Rock, holding him high above his head for all to see— Simba, their new prince and future king.

Across the plains, Mufasa's brother, Scar, trapped a helpless mouse under his paw. "Life's not fair, is it? You see, I shall never be king. And you . . . shall never see the light of another day," he said as he dangled the mouse over his open mouth.

"Didn't your mother ever tell you not to play with your food?" the king's advisor, Zazu, interrupted.

"What do you want?" Scar demanded.

"I'm here to announce that King Mufasa's on his way," Zazu explained, "so you'd better have a good excuse for missing the ceremony this morning."

"Oooh," said Scar sarcastically, "I quiver with fear." He launched at Zazu, trapping him in his mouth.

"Scar!" Mufasa yelled from the entrance of the lair. "Drop him."

"Impeccable timing, Your Majesty," said Zazu.

Mufasa strode toward Scar. "Sarabi and I didn't see you at the presentation of Simba."

Zazu hopped forward. "As the king's brother, you should have been first in line."

"Well, I *was* first in line until the little hairball was born," replied Scar.

"That hairball is my son and your future king," said Mufasa.

"Oh, I shall practice my curtsy," said Scar, turning away.

"Don't turn your back on me, Scar."

"Oh, no, Mufasa. Perhaps you shouldn't turn your back on *me*," hissed Scar.

"Is that a challenge?" roared Mufasa.

"I wouldn't dream of challenging you. As far as brains go, I got the lion's share. But when it comes to brute strength, I'm afraid I'm at the shallow end of the gene pool."

And with those words, he walked away.

That night, as the rains fell and lightning crackled through the sky, Rafiki stood beneath the branches of a tree. He painted a picture of a lion cub on the bark.

"Simba," he said with a smile.

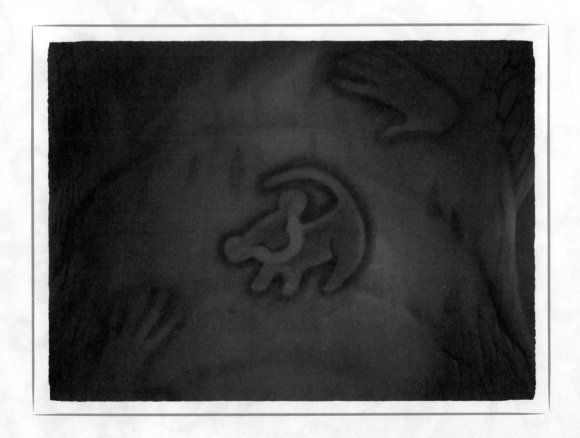

As the months passed, Simba grew into a curious cub, running all over Pride Rock. One morning, before dawn, he ran to his father. "Dad! Dad! Dad! Dad!" he called to Mufasa, nudging him. "Come on, Dad! You promised!"

"Okay, okay, I'm up, I'm up," said Mufasa.

He led Simba to the edge of Pride Rock to watch the dawn light break across the sky. "Look, Simba. Everything the light touches is our kingdom," said Mufasa. "A king's time as ruler rises and falls like the sun. One day, Simba, the sun will set on my time here and will rise with you as the new king."

"And this'll all be mine?" gasped Simba.

"Everything," said Mufasa.

"What about that shadowy place?" asked Simba.

"That's beyond our borders," Mufasa replied. "You must never go there, Simba."

Together, father and son began to walk across the plains, with Zazu flying behind them. "Everything you see exists together in a delicate balance," explained Mufasa. "As king, you need to understand that balance and respect all the creatures, from the crawling ant to the leaping antelope."

"But, Dad, don't we eat the antelope?"

"Yes, Simba, but let me explain. When we die, our bodies become the grass, and the antelope eat the grass. And so we are all connected in the great Circle of Life."

"Sire!" called Zazu urgently. "Hyenas in the Pride Lands!"

Mufasa tensed. "Zazu, take Simba home," he ordered. Without a moment's delay, he ran toward the Pride Lands.

"I never get to go anywhere," grumbled Simba, watching his father leave.

While Mufasa dealt with the hyenas, Simba visited his uncle Scar at his rocky lair. "I'm gonna be king of Pride Rock," he announced. "My dad just showed me the whole kingdom. And I'm gonna rule it all."

"So your father showed you the whole kingdom, did he?" asked Scar.

"Everything," said Simba.

"He didn't show you what's beyond that rise at the northern border?"

"Well . . . no," admitted Simba. "He said I can't go there."

"And he's absolutely right. It's far too dangerous," agreed Scar. "Only the bravest lions go there."

"Well, I'm brave," said Simba. "What's out there?"

"I'm sorry, Simba. I just can't tell you. An elephant graveyard is no place for a young prince. Oops!" Scar clapped his paw over his mouth.

"Whoa!" said Simba.

"Promise me you'll never visit that dreadful place," said Scar. "You run along now and have fun. And remember, it's our little secret."

As Simba left, an evil smile crept across Scar's face.

Simba ran to his friend Nala who was getting bathed by her mother. "Come on. I just heard about this great place," he said. "It's really cool."

"So where is this really cool place?" asked Simba's mother, Sarabi.

"Oh," said Simba, "around the water hole . . ."

Simba gave Nala a secret look, and then they both said, "Please!"

"As long as Zazu goes with you," said Sarabi.

"So where are we *really* going?" whispered Nala as they began their journey.

"An elephant graveyard," Simba whispered back.

"Wow!" said Nala. "So how are we going to ditch the dodo?"

Simba grinned. They created a distraction with help from a herd of animals.

"We lost him!" said Nala.

"I . . . am a genius," Simba boasted.

"Hey, genius," Nala replied. "It was my idea." The cubs playfully pounced on each other. Nala pinned Simba to the ground.

They began tumbling over each other, down a rocky slope, until they landed with a thud in the Elephant Graveyard.

"It's really creepy," said Nala.

"Yeah," agreed Simba. "Let's go check it out."

But at that moment, Zazu flew down. "The only 'checking out' you will do will be to check out of here. We're way beyond the boundary of the Pride Lands," he squawked. "Right now, we are all in very real danger."

"Danger? Ha!" said Simba. "I walk on the wild side. I laugh in the face of danger." He let out a laugh.

But his laughter was drowned out by the sound of three hyenas laughing.

"Well, well, well," said Shenzi. "What have we got here?"

"A trio of trespassers!" replied Banzai as the third hyena, Ed, continued to laugh.

Then Shenzi turned to Zazu. "I know you. You're Mufasa's little stooge."

"It's time to go!" insisted Zazu.

"What's the hurry?" asked Shenzi. "We'd love you to stick around for *dinner*."

"Yeah," said Banzai. "We could have whatever's *lion* around!"

With that, Nala and Simba ran. The cubs ran until they were trapped against a wall. They turned to see the hyenas stalking toward them.

Suddenly, Mufasa leaped down, pinning the hyenas to the ground.

"If you ever come near my son again . . ." Mufasa growled.

The hyenas fled. They were no match for Mufasa.

"Dad, I—" Simba began.

"You deliberately disobeyed me. Let's go home," Mufasa said sternly.

While Zazu took Nala home, Mufasa turned to his son. "Simba, I'm very disappointed in you."

"I was just trying to be brave, like you," said Simba.

"I'm only brave when I have to be," explained Mufasa.

"But you're not scared of anything."

"I was today," said Mufasa. "I thought I might lose you."

"I guess even kings get scared, huh?"

Mufasa smiled down at his son. "Come here, you," he said. He picked Simba up, ruffling his head. Then they rolled together through the moonlit grass.

"Dad?" said Simba. "We're pals, right?"

"Right," answered Mufasa.

"And we'll always be together, right?"

Mufasa paused for a moment. "Let me tell you something that my father told me. Look at the stars. The great kings of the past look down on us from those stars. So whenever you feel alone, just remember that those kings will always be there to guide you. And so will I."

Meanwhile, Scar visited the hyenas.

"Hey, did you bring us anything to eat?" asked Banzai.

"I don't think you really deserve this," said Scar, holding up a zebra's leg. "I practically gift-wrapped those cubs for you, and you couldn't even dispose of them."

"It wasn't exactly like they were alone, Scar," said the hyenas. "What were we supposed to do? Kill Mufasa?"

"Precisely," said Scar.

The next day, Scar took Simba down to the gorge. "Now you wait here," he instructed. "Your father has a *marvelous* surprise for you."

"Hey, Uncle Scar. Will I like this surprise?"

"Simba," said Scar as he turned to leave, "it's to *die* for."

On the grasslands above the gorge, a herd of wildebeests were peacefully gathered while the hyenas hid behind a rock. On Scar's signal, they startled the wildebeests, driving them down into the gorge.

The first thing Simba felt was the ground trembling beneath him. Then he saw the powerful stampede rushing toward him. Simba would be trampled in an instant! In terror, he ran.

Scar had reached Mufasa. "Quick! Stampede in the gorge. Simba's down there!"

As Mufasa ran to save his son, Simba clung to a low branch. The stampede raced past him.

"Your father is on the way," Zazu cried. "Hold on!"

But Simba's branch was beginning to break. "Dad!" he screamed.

Mufasa leaped into the gorge and ran through the stampede until he grabbed his son. Then he placed Simba on a rocky ledge. A moment later, Mufasa was struck by a wildebeest and dragged into the stampede.

Mufasa clawed his way back up the rocks. When he reached the top, he called out to Scar for help.

Scar reached down and gouged his claws into Mufasa's outstretched paws just out of Simba's view. "Long live the king," he said with menace as he threw Mufasa back down into the gorge.

"No!" yelled Simba as he caught sight of his father falling.

By the time Simba reached the bottom of the gorge, the herd was gone. In the dusty air, he found his father, lying on the ground.

"You've got to get up," cried Simba. But Mufasa did not move.

"Help!" called Simba as tears slid down his face. "Somebody, anybody, help."

He crept under his father's paw and lay there until Scar arrived.

"Simba," said Scar. "What have you done? The king is dead. And if it weren't for you, he'd still be alive. What will your mother think?"

"What am I going to do?" asked Simba, sobbing.

"Run away, Simba," said Scar. "Run. Run away and never return."

And at those words, Simba ran.

Behind Scar, the hyenas were waiting. "Kill him," commanded Scar.

The hyenas chased Simba until they came to a large patch of thorny bushes. Only Simba could fit through without getting scratched.

"There ain't no way I'm going in there," said Shenzi, not wanting to get pricked by the thorns. "He's as good as dead out there anyway. And if he comes back, we'll kill him."

On Pride Rock, Scar stood before the other lions.
"Mufasa's death is a terrible tragedy," he said. "But to lose
Simba, who had barely begun to live . . . for me, it is a deep,
personal loss. So it is with a heavy heart that I assume the
throne. Yet out of the ashes of this tragedy, we shall rise to
greet the dawning of a new era, in which lion and hyena
come together in a great and glorious future."

As he spoke, the hyenas crowded onto Pride Rock, their howling laughter echoing over the land.

Standing beside his tree, Rafiki shook his head in sorrow. Then he raised his paw and smeared his picture of Simba.

Far away, on dry, cracked ground, Simba lay sleeping, encircled by vultures. Then the sound of hooves filled the air as Pumbaa the warthog and his friend Timon the meerkat barreled into them.

"I love it! Bowling for buzzards!" said Pumbaa as the vultures scattered. "Hey, Timon, you better come look. I think it's still alive."

Timon sniffed Simba and lifted his paw. "Jeez, it's a lion!" he cried. "Run, Pumbaa. Move it!"

"Hey, Timon, it's just a little lion. Look at him. He's so cute and all alone. Can we keep him?"

"Lions eat guys like us!"

"Maybe he'll be on our side!" said Pumbaa.

"Hey! I got it!" said Timon. "What if he's on our side? You know, having a lion around might not be such a bad idea."

Pumbaa bent down, scooped up the sleeping Simba with his tusks, and carried him away.

They laid Simba down beneath a tree and splashed him with water until he woke up.

"I saved you," said Timon. "Well, Pumbaa helped. A little."

"Thanks for your help," said Simba, and he began to walk away.

"Hey, where you going?" asked Timon.

"Nowhere," said Simba.

"So, where you from?" asked Timon, running after him.

"Who cares?" said Simba. "I can't go back."

"You're an outcast," said Timon. "That's great, so are we."

"What did you do, kid?" asked Pumbaa.

"Something terrible. But I don't want to talk about it."

"You know, kid," said Pumbaa, "in times like this, my buddy Timon here says, 'You got to put your behind in your past.'"

"No, no, no. Amateur, lie down before you hurt yourself. It's, 'You got to put your past behind you,'" said Timon. "Repeat after me: hakuna matata."

"What?" asked Simba.

"It means 'no worries,'" explained Pumbaa.

Simba followed his new friends to their home. When it was time to eat, Timon offered a slimy grub to Simba, who took it reluctantly.

"Oh, well," said Simba, holding up the grub. "Hakuna matata."

The days passed, and then the months, and the years. Soon Simba was a full-grown lion, living in a worry-free paradise with his friends.

But back at Pride Rock, the animals were living through dark days. Even the hyenas were complaining.

"Scar," said Shenzi. "There's no food, no water."

"I thought things were bad under Mufasa," said Banzai.

"What did you say?" snarled Scar. "Get out!"

Meanwhile, Simba, Pumbaa, and Timon were lying on their backs, gazing up at the starry night sky.

"Ever wonder what those sparkly dots are up there?" asked Pumbaa.

"Well," said Simba reluctantly, "somebody once told me that the great kings of the past are up there, watching over us."

"You mean a bunch of royal dead guys are watching us?" said Timon. He and Pumbaa started to laugh.

"Yeah," said Simba, pretending to laugh with them. "Pretty dumb, huh?" He walked over to a ledge and flopped down, sending a cloud of dust swirling away on the breeze.

On the other side of the plains, Rafiki caught the dust in his hands and examined it. "Simba?" he said. "He's . . . he's alive? He's alive!" Then he painted a new picture of Simba on the trunk of his tree. "It is time," he announced.

Unaware of Rafiki's discovery, Nala, now a fully grown lioness, was searching for food. As she stalked through the grasses, she caught Pumbaa's scent and gave chase. But as she pounced to catch him, Simba leaped at her with a roar.

They rolled over and over until Nala pinned Simba to the ground, just like she had when they were cubs.

"Nala?" said Simba. "Is it really you?"

Nala drew back. "Who are you?" she asked.

"It's me. Simba."

For a moment she froze; then she smiled. "Whoa! How did you . . . ? Where did you come from?" she asked.

"It's great to see you," said Simba.

"Hey! What's goin' on here?" cried Timon, coming between them.

"Timon, this is Nala. She's my best friend."

"Wait till everyone finds out you've been here all this time," said Nala. "And your mother . . . what will she think?"

"She doesn't have to know," said Simba. "Nobody has to know."

"Of course they do. Everyone thinks you're dead. Scar told us about the stampede."

"He did? What else did he tell you?"

"What else matters? You're alive. And that means . . . you're the king," said Nala. "You don't know how much this will mean to everyone. What it means to me. I've really missed you."

"I've missed you, too," said Simba.

And they walked off together, drinking from pools and bounding through the grasses. Nala became confused.

"We've really needed you at home," said Nala. "You're the king."

"Scar is," replied Simba.

"Simba, he let the hyenas take over the Pride Lands. Everything's destroyed. There's no food. No water. If you don't do something soon, everyone will starve."

"I can't go back," Simba said. "Look, sometimes bad things happen and there's nothing you can do about it. So why worry?"

"Because it's your responsibility," Nala explained. "Don't you understand? You're our only hope."

"Sorry," said Simba, hanging his head.

"What's happened to you? You're not the Simba I remember."

"Listen," Simba said. "You think you can just show up and tell me how to live my life? You don't even know what I've been through." Then he walked away.

As darkness covered the sky, Simba gazed up at the stars. "You said you'd always be there for me. But you're not. And it's because of me. It's my fault," he said, choking back tears.

Then Simba heard chanting coming from the treetops.

It was Rafiki. "I know who you are," he said, leaping down from a tree. "You're Mufasa's boy."

Simba turned to Rafiki in wonder.

"He's alive! And I'll show him to you," Rafiki said, darting away.

Simba raced after him through twisted tree branches and vines.

Rafiki suddenly stopped at a pool of water. Simba looked down, but only saw his reflection.

"Look harder," said Rafiki.

This time, Mufasa appeared to gaze back at Simba. "You see," said Rafiki. "He lives in you."

"Simba," called Mufasa's voice from the clouds.

Simba looked up at the sky, and there was Mufasa, surrounded by a billowing cloud. "Look inside yourself, Simba. You are more than what you have become. You must take your place in the Circle of Life. Remember who you are. You are my son and the one true king."

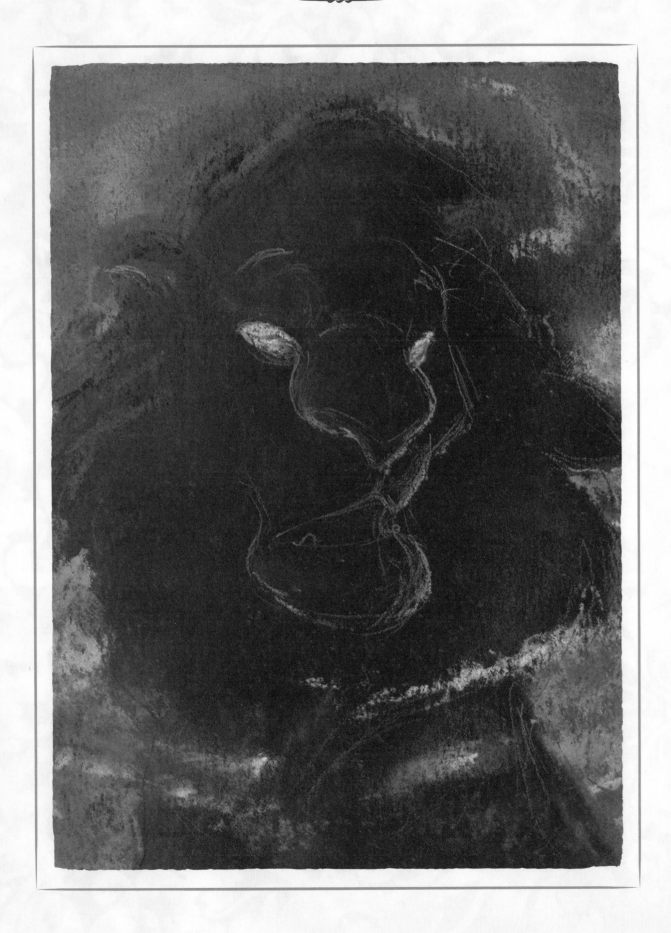

Then his image faded and Simba was alone again with Rafiki.

"I know what I have to do, but going back means I'll have to face my past," Simba said.

Rafiki took his stick and whacked Simba on the head.

"Ow, geez, what was that for?" Simba asked.

"It doesn't matter, it's in the past," Rafiki explained.

"Yeah, but it still hurts."

"Oh, yes, the past can hurt," said Rafiki. "But the way I see it, you can either run from it, or learn from it." And at that, he went to whack Simba on the head again—only this time, Simba avoided it.

With that, Simba took off. He ran all the way back to the Pride Lands. When he arrived, he looked around in shock at the barren land.

"It's awful, isn't it?" asked Nala. She had just arrived, too. "What made you come back?"

"This is my kingdom," said Simba. "If I don't fight for it, who will?"

As they neared Pride Rock, they weren't alone. Pumbaa and Timon had joined them and were now distracting the hyenas with a song and dance while Simba and Nala snuck past them.

Simba saw his mother standing before Scar. "There is nothing left," Sarabi told Scar. "We have only one choice. We must leave Pride Rock."

"We're not going anywhere," said Scar.

"Then you have sentenced us to death."

"I am the king," replied Scar. "I can do whatever I want."

"If you were half the king Mufasa was—" Sarabi began, but Scar knocked her to the ground before she could finish.

"I am ten times the king Mufasa was!"

There was a snarling sound and Scar looked up to see Simba. He raced down to his mother.

"Simba?" said Sarabi.

"I'm home," said Simba, touching his head to hers.

"Simba," purred Scar. "I'm a little surprised to see you . . . alive."

"Step down, Scar," demanded Simba.

"There is one little problem," said Scar. "You see them?" He pointed to the hyenas. "They think *I'm* king."

"Well, we don't," said Nala. "Simba's the rightful king."

"Ah," said Scar, circling Simba. "So, you haven't told them your little secret. Well, Simba, now's your chance to tell them. Tell them who is responsible for Mufasa's death."

"I am," said Simba.

"You see? He admits it. Murderer!" cried Scar.

"No, it was an accident," explained Simba.

"If it weren't for you, Mufasa would still be alive," retorted Scar. "It's your fault he's dead. Do you deny it?"

"No," replied Simba.

"Then you're guilty!" Scar said, seething.

Scar drove Simba back toward the edge of the rock. "Oh, Simba," he went on. "You're in trouble again. But this time, Daddy isn't here to save you, and now everyone knows why!"

Simba slipped and fell. He clung to the edge of the rock. A spark of lightning struck the dry grasses below him, which burst into flame.

"Now this looks familiar," said Scar. "This is just the way your father looked before he died." Then he bent down close. "And here's my little secret," he whispered. "I . . . killed . . . Mufasa."

Simba sprung up, pinning Scar to the ground while the hyenas and lionesses watched. "Murderer!" he shouted. "Tell them the truth."

"I did it," Scar whispered.

"So they can hear you," demanded Simba.

"I killed Mufasa," admitted Scar.

Realizing the moment had come, the hyenas sprang at the lionesses, who fought back with the help of Simba's friends.

Simba gave chase to Scar, who tried to run away. "Murderer," growled Simba. "You don't deserve to live."

"But, Simba, I am family. It's the hyenas who are the real enemy. It was their fault. It was their idea."

"Why should I believe you? Everything you ever told me was a lie," replied Simba.

"What are you going to do? You wouldn't kill your own uncle."

"No, Scar. I'm not like you," said Simba. "Run. Run away, Scar, and *never* return."

But as Scar prowled past Simba, he threw burning coals into Simba's eyes and leaped at him.

The two lions fought, pounding with their paws and slashing with their claws. At last, Simba sent Scar tumbling over the cliff's edge.

Scar rose slowly to his feet just as the hyenas approached him. "My friends," said Scar.

"Friends?" said Shenzi. "I thought he said we were the enemy."

Then they set upon him as flames consumed the land.

Soon rain fell from the sky, extinguishing the flames. Simba and the lionesses gathered beneath Pride Rock. "It is time," said Rafiki to Simba.

Simba walked to the top of Pride Rock. He gazed up at the rain clouds. "Remember," his father's voice boomed. Then Simba let out a deep roar that echoed across the plains. He had taken his place as king.

In time, the Pride Lands were green again. The herds returned. Simba stood on Pride Rock with Nala, Timon, and Pumbaa beside him, while Zazu circled above. The animals of the Pride Lands bowed low before them as Rafiki walked to the edge of Pride Rock, holding Simba and Nala's cub in his hands. He held the lion cub high above his head in celebration of the Circle of Life.

And they lived . . .

happily ever after.

The End

The Art of Disney's The Lion King

The Lion King was Disney's first original feature animation film not based on source material. The concept for a coming-of-age tale set in Africa was born on a plane ride and, through research trips and intensive brain storming sessions, the film we now know began to emerge. The artists working on the film were inspired by African art, as well as by the actors cast in the film. Animators attended lectures on animal movement and behavior and had the opportunity to sketch from live animals, brought into the studio. *The Lion King* is often praised for its artistic brilliance, and throughout this book you can see concept art, animation cels, and story sketches from the following Disney Studio artists.

Dan Cooper

After graduating from the Art Center College of Design and a stint in advertising, Dan Cooper joined the Walt Disney Studios in 1990 working on films such as *Aladdin*, *The Lion King*, and *Pocahontas* as a background artist. Cooper now works as a visual development artist and has contributed to some of Disney's most recent animated films including *Tangled*, *Moana*, *Wreck-It Ralph*, and *Ralph Breaks the Internet*.
Background painting on page 17.

Bob Smith

Bob Smith is a California native, and he's worked for the U.S. Navy and as a fine artist, but he spent more than forty years in animation. Smith joined the Walt Disney Studios as a layout artist and character designer on films including *Oliver & Company*, *The Rescuers Down Under*, and *The Lion King*.
Concept art on page 18.

Don Moore

Don Moore is principally a background artist who has contributed to many Disney animated features, including *The Lion King*, *Pocahontas*, *The Hunchback of Notre Dame*, *Hercules*, and *Tarzan*.
Color key on page 26.

Roger Allers

Inspired by a childhood love of Disney, Roger Allers joined the Walt Disney Studios in 1985 as a storyboard artist for *Oliver & Company*. Allers continued to work on story boarding for films such as *The Little Mermaid* and *The Rescuers Down Under* before undertaking the role of head of story on *Beauty and the Beast*. In 1991, Allers signed on to co-direct a project titled *King of the Jungle* which later became *The Lion King*. Allers went on to co-write the libretto for *The Lion King* on Broadway, for which he received a Tony nomination.
Story sketch on page 21.

Chris Sanders

A CalArts alum, Chris Sanders joined the Walt Disney Studios shortly after graduation in 1984. Sanders has worked as a character designer, storyboard artist, artistic director, and production designer across projects such as *Beauty and the Beast*, *The Lion King*, and *Mulan*. Sanders directed the 2002 animation *Lilo & Stitch* and also provided the voice of Stitch for many of the Western releases of the film.
Concept art on pages 22, 40, and 43; story sketch on page 57.

———— ❧ ————

Lisa Keene

Joining the Walt Disney Studios in 1982, Lisa Keene has worked as a visual development artist and background supervisor on some of Disney's most beloved films including *Beauty and the Beast*, *The Lion King*, *Enchanted*, *The Princess and the Frog*, and *Tangled*.

Color key on page 83.

Rick Maki

Canadian-born animator Rick Maki joined the Walt Disney Studios to work in the story department for *The Lion King*. Maki has worked as a character designer and visual development artist on many Disney features including *Hercules*, *Tarzan*, and *The Princess and the Frog*.

Concept art on page 23.

Dave Burgess

Animator Dave Burgess has worked on many Disney films, animating characters such as Genie in *Aladdin*, Gaston in *Beauty and the Beast*, Jane in *Tarzan*, and Milo in *Atlantis: The Lost Empire*. For *The Lion King*, Burgess worked as the supervising animator for the hyenas.

Concept art on page 27.

Lorna Cook

Lorna Cook worked as an animator and storyboard artist at the Walt Disney Studios throughout the 1980s and 1990s, contributing to films such as *The Fox and the Hound*, *Beauty and the Beast*, and *Mulan*. For *The Lion King*, Cook animated adult Simba.

Story sketch on page 28 and 30.

Andy Gaskill

At twenty-one, Andy Gaskill joined the Walt Disney Studios straight from art school, where he enrolled in the first animation training program, supervised by Disney veteran Eric Larson. Gaskill first worked as an animator on *Winnie the Pooh and Tigger Too*, *The Rescuers*, and *The Fox and the Hound* before moving into roles such as storyboard artist for *TRON*, visual development artist for *The Little Mermaid*, and art director for *The Lion King*, *Hercules*, and *Treasure Planet*. Gaskill also worked for Walt Disney's Imagineering, creating designs for attractions at the Walt Disney Parks and Resorts.

Story sketch on pages 31, 56, 58, 59, and 61.

———— ❧ ————

Doug Ball

Working as a background artist and visual development artist, Doug Ball has contributed to some of Disney's most popular films of the 1990s and 2000s, including *Beauty and the Beast*, *The Lion King*, *Enchanted*, and *The Princess and the Frog*.

Color key on page 34; concept art on page 50 and 53.

Greg Drolette

Greg Drolette worked at the Walt Disney Studios during the 1980s and 1990s, creating background paintings for some of the biggest films of this period including *The Little Mermaid*, *Beauty and the Beast*, *Aladdin*, *The Lion King*, *Hercules* and *Atlantis: The Lost Empire*.

Background painting on pages 2-3 and 78-79; color key on page 72.

Mark Henn

In 1978, Mark Henn studied in the Walt Disney Character Animation program at CalArts and was hired at the Walt Disney Studios in 1980. His first big assignment was to animate Mickey Mouse in *Mickey's Christmas Carol* —since then he has worked on dozens of Disney's biggest films, specializing in animating female characters such as Ariel in *The Little Mermaid*, Belle in *Beauty and the Beast*, Jasmine in *Aladdin*, the titlular character of *Mulan*, Tiana in *The Princess and the Frog*, and Anna in *Frozen*. For *The Lion King*, Mark worked as the supervising animator for young Simba.

Concept art on page 33.

Thom Enriquez

Thom Enriquez is a story board artist and animator who contributed to the story development of films such as *The Lion King*, *Hercules*, *Mulan*, and *Brother Bear*. Enriquez has also worked on *Beauty and the Beast*, *The Hunchback of Notre Dame*, and *The Little Mermaid*.

Concept art on page 7; story sketch on page 35.

Anthony DeRosa

Anthony "Tony" DeRosa has worked at the Walt Disney Studios since 1985, working as an animator on films such as *The Little Mermaid*, *Beauty and the Beast*, and *Aladdin*. For *The Lion King*, DeRosa was the supervising animator for adult Nala.

Concept art on page 51.

Hans Bacher

Hans Bacher, born in Germany, is a well-known and respected animation artist. He began his Disney career in 1987 and has worked as a production designer, visual development artist, storyboard artist and character designer on films including *Aladdin*, *Beauty and the Beast*, *The Lion King*, *Hercules*, and *Mulan*.

Concept art on pages 8-9.

Andreas Deja

Polish-born animator Andreas Deja joined the Walt Disney Studios animation department in 1980 and quickly established himself as a supervising animator for some of the most memorable Disney villains. He has animated Gaston in *Beauty and the Beast*, Jafar in *Aladdin*, and Scar in *The Lion King*. Deja doesn't always animate the bad guys! For *The Little Mermaid*, Deja animated King Triton as well as the titular character from *Hercules*, Lilo in *Lilo & Stitch*, and Tigger in the 2011 animated feature *Winnie the Pooh*. In 2015, Deja was named a Disney Legend.

Concept art on pages 14, 32, 38, 63, and 64; rough animation drawing on page 48.

Tony Bancroft

Best known for co-directing *Mulan*, Tony Bancroft has animated some of Disney's most memorable sidekicks including Cogsworth in *Beauty and the Beast*, Iago in *Aladdin*, Pumbaa in *The Lion King*, and Kronk in *The Emperor's New Groove*.

Concept art on page 42 with Michael Surrey.

Ellen Woodbury

Joining Disney in the 1980s, Ellen Woodbury spent twenty years of her career working as an animator across many of Disney's biggest films of the period. Following an MFA in Experimental Animation at CalArts and a short stint at another studio, Woodbury joined the Walt Disney Studios and apprenticed under Mike Gabriel, Hendel Butoy, and Mark Henn. Woodbury became the first female supervising animator, a role which she began on *The Lion King*, supervising the animation of Zazu.

Animation drawing on page 16.

Barry Johnson

Story board and visual development artist Barry Johnson has worked across many Disney films including *The Lion King* and *Mulan*. Most recently Johnson has contributed to *Big Hero 6*, *Wreck-It Ralph*, *Frozen*, and *Moana*, as well as Pixar Animation Studio's *Brave*.

Story sketch on pages 36, 44, and 49.

Tom Shannon

Tom Shannon worked as a layout artist for two decades at the Walt Disney Studios, contributing to films such as *The Rescuers Down Under*, *Beauty and the Beast*, *Aladdin*, *The Lion King*, *Mulan*, and *Tarzan*.

Concept art on page 69.

Burny Mattinson

Working with the Walt Disney Studios for more than sixty-five years, Burny Mattinson has almost done it all. Starting with the company in 1953, Mattinson has been an animator, story artist, writer, director, and producer for over half a century of Disney classics such as *Sleeping Beauty*, *The Jungle Book*, *The Rescuers*, *Mickey's Christmas Carol*, *The Great Mouse Detective*, *The Little Mermaid*, *Aladdin*, *The Lion King*, and *Big Hero 6*, among others. His continuing love of the medium of animation and for the simple joys of storytelling are an inspiration to filmmakers and audiences around the world.

Story sketch on pages 39 and 45.

Michael Surrey

Michael Surrey moved to California from Canada following the release of *The Little Mermaid* to join the Walt Disney Studios. He was hired as an assistant animator on *Beauty and the Beast* and went on to assist Glen Keane in his animation of the titular character of *Aladdin*. For *The Lion King*, Surrey was assigned as supervising animator for the meerkat, Timon. Following that success, Surrey worked as a supervising animator on many Disney characters including Terk in *Tarzan* and Ray in *The Princess and the Frog*.

Concept art on page 42 with Tony Bancroft and page 81.

Kelvin Yasuda

Joining the Walt Disney Studios in the 1980s, Kelvin Yasuda contributed to many Disney films of the 1980s, 1990s, and 2000s as an effects animator. Yasuda worked on *The Black Cauldron*, *Oliver & Company*, *The Little Mermaid*, *Beauty and the Beast*, *The Lion King*, and *Fantasia/2000*.

Concept art on page 68.

Glossary of Terms

Animation drawing: an illustration created for the final animation, ready to be traced on to a cel.

Background painting: establishes the color, style, and mood of a scene. They're combined with cels for cel set-ups or for the finished scene.

Cel: a sheet of clear celluloid, on which animation drawings are traced using ink and painted with color. To create a finished frame of a scene, the cel is photographed against the background painting, which shows through the unpainted areas. Though they were not created for the making of *The Lion King*, special cels were created as physical reference of the ink and paint colors of the characters.

Color key: establishes the look and feel of a background painting and overall color of a scene. Color keys help animators avoid any color overlaps or clashes when placing characters and objects on backgrounds.

Concept art: drawings, paintings or sketches prepared in the early stages of a film's development. Concept art is often used to inspire the staging, mood, and atmosphere of scenes.

Rough animation drawing: a drawing created very early in the animation process to test an animation.

Story sketch: shows the action that's happening in a scene, as well as presenting the emotion of the story moment. Story sketches help visualize the film before expensive resources are committed to its production.